For Alexis & Rose

For further information, contact:
Tumblehome, Inc.
201 Newbury St, Suite 201
Boston, MA 02116
http://tumblehomebooks.org/

Library of Congress Control Number 2019940377
ISBN-13 978-1-943431-51-9
ISBN-10 1-943431-51-5

Lee, Ingrid
The Shooing Cave / Ingrid Lee - 1st ed
Illustrated by Johnny Hollick


Printed in Taiwan
10 9 8 7 6 5 4 3 2 1

# THE SHOOING CAVE

WRITTEN BY INGRID LEE   ILLUSTRATED BY JOHNNY HOLLICK

A little boy looked out his window.

*"Daddy, Daddy,"* the boy whispered. *"I hear something!"*

*"Hmmm,"* his father answered.

*"Maybe the night wind is dusting the treetops."*

*"No, Daddy.  It's not that."*

*"Maybe the river is scrubbing the caves."*

*"No, Daddy!  It's not that either."*

*"Maybe the Stark is singing a lullaby."*

*"Yes!"*   The little boy laughed.  *"Tell me the story!"*

*"Well,"* said his father, *"this is what I remember..."*

The Stark lives in the caves.
Every day he looks for treasure.

Caves are chilly.
One day the Stark put a bead of ice in his pouch.
When he looked for it later, it was gone.

Caves have no doors.
Once, the Stark put a caterpillar in his pouch.
But in a few days, it flew away.

Another time, the Stark took a cave painting back to his nest.
His paws grew dusty trying to find it again.

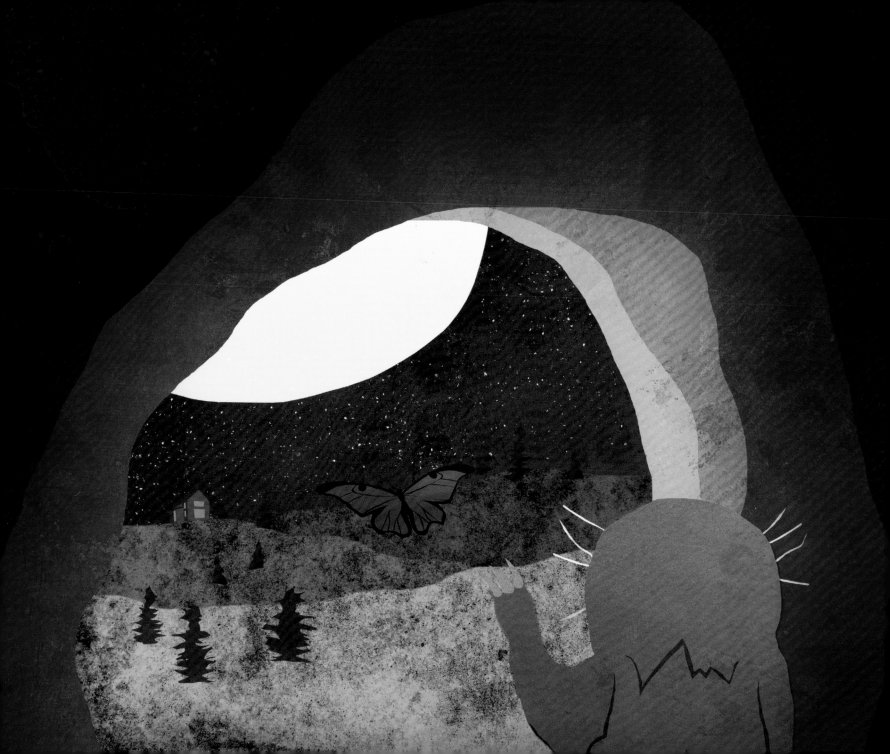

The Stark is a handsome fellow.
Short blue hairs cover his body.
Underneath, the hairs are silver.
His eyes are black buttons
swimming in pools of milk.

The Stark keeps his eyes
closed most of the time.
Caves are too dark for eyes.

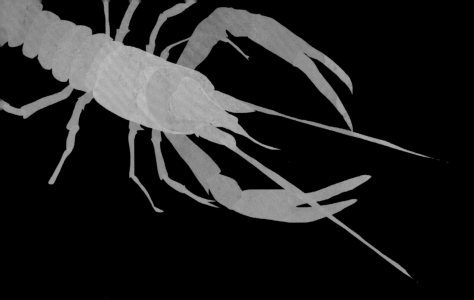

Every day the Stark listens to plinks and plops.
He sniffs at the blind crayfish hiding in the shallows.
He dips a furry foot into the mirror pond.

One night he saw a bright light.
The Stark thought the sun had rolled into the cave.

A boy sat by a fire.
The boy was used to small hard places and deep, dark pools.
But he had never seen a handsome, silver Stark.
He didn't believe his eyes.

"*Shoo!*" He waved his fire-poking stick. "*Shoo!*"

The boy crawled into his sleeping bag.
I'm dreaming, he thought.

"*Shoo!*"

In the morning the boy turned on his headlight.
He put matches and candles in his bag.
He packed rope and orange markers.
Then he walked deep into the cave.

A cave is darker than a night without stars.

Caving is hard work.
Sometimes the boy had to squeeze
through an opening as thin as a tiger's eye.
Sometimes he had to slide down a slope as
slippery as a whale's back.

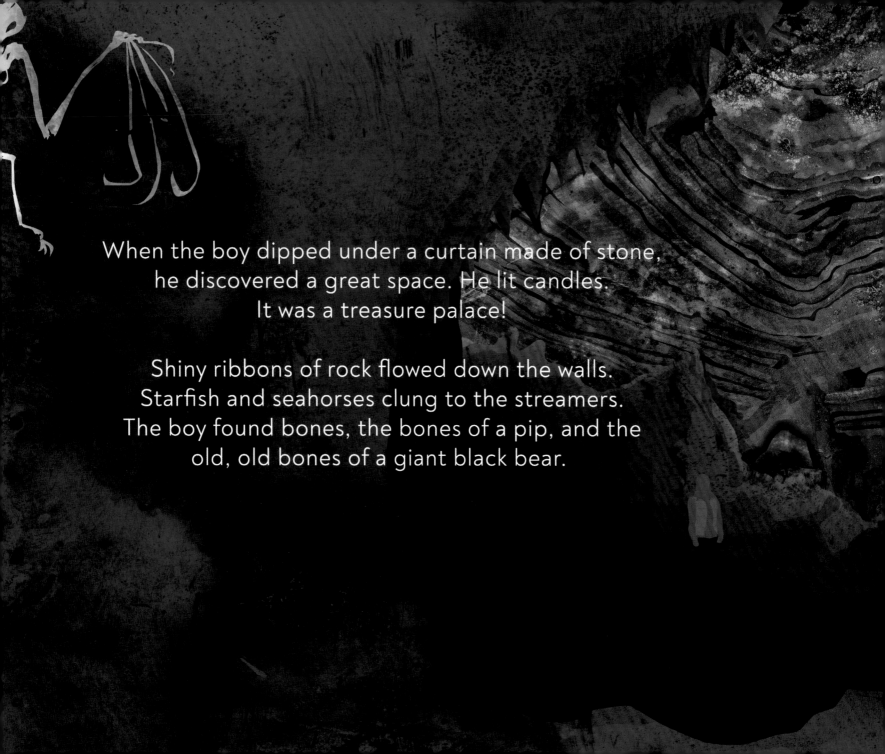

When the boy dipped under a curtain made of stone,
he discovered a great space. He lit candles.
It was a treasure palace!

Shiny ribbons of rock flowed down the walls.
Starfish and seahorses clung to the streamers.
The boy found bones, the bones of a pip, and the
old, old bones of a giant black bear.

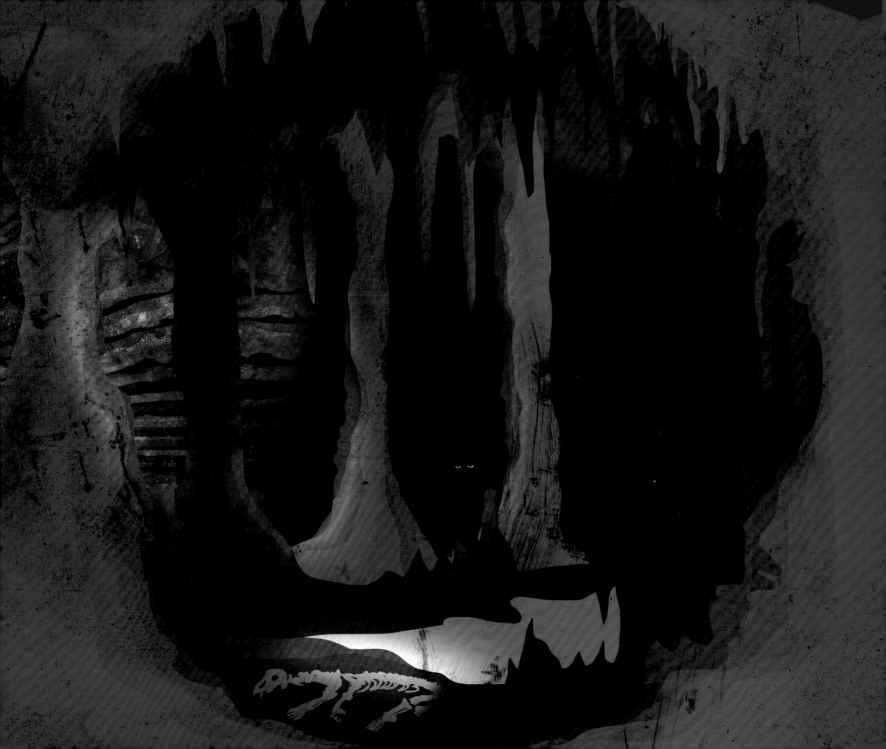

The boy lit candles.
He drew dragon teeth and walrus whiskers.
He took pictures of the rock roses.

There was a nest too.  The nest was too big!

Something blue reflected in the water.

The boy went back to his fire to rest. He warmed his hands.

The Stark peeped out of the cave.

"*Shoo,*" the boy hissed. "*I don't see you. Shoo!*"

Every day the boy explored the caves.
Every day the Stark searched for treasure.
Once, where the tunnel walls were thin as
paper, they passed each other.
*"You're not there,"* said the boy. *"Shoo!"*

The boy sat by the fire every night.
Every night the Stark watched.
Finally the boy stamped his foot.
*"I'm going home tomorrow,"* he said. *"So shoo!"*

The Stark pulled something from his pouch.
His nose twitched. *"Shoo!"* he sneezed.
A stone pearl fell to the ground.
It rolled right up to the boy's foot.

*"Shoo!"*

The Stark ran away, chasing
his own voice down the tunnel.

The boy looked at the pearl for a long time.

The boy took off his vest.
With his fire-poking stick, he drew two shapes.
He cut out the shapes and sewed them together again.
The stitches were small and tight.

He used his hair to stuff the toy.
The buttons from his shirt made a pair of shiny eyes.

"*Shoo!*" the Stark whispered from inside the cave.

"*Shoo,*" said the boy. "*Shoo Shoooo!*"

They talked all night long.

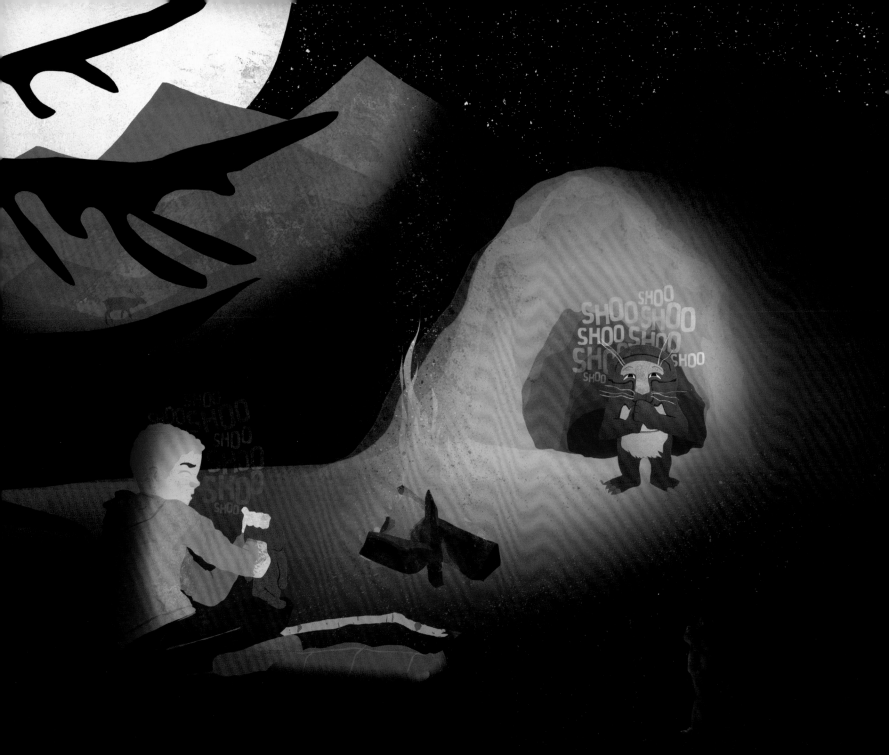

At dawn, the Stark found his nest.

The boy packed his things and left the cave.

Later, when the Stark crept back to the fire,
it was cold.

*"Shoo?"* he whispered.  *"Shoo?"*

There was nobody to answer.

But something waited in the ashes.

A gift!

It was a small, blue baby.

*"Shoooooo..."* the Stark whispered.

It was a baby Stark!

*"Shoo,"* the Stark said.

*"Shooo Shoo, Shooo Shoo!"*

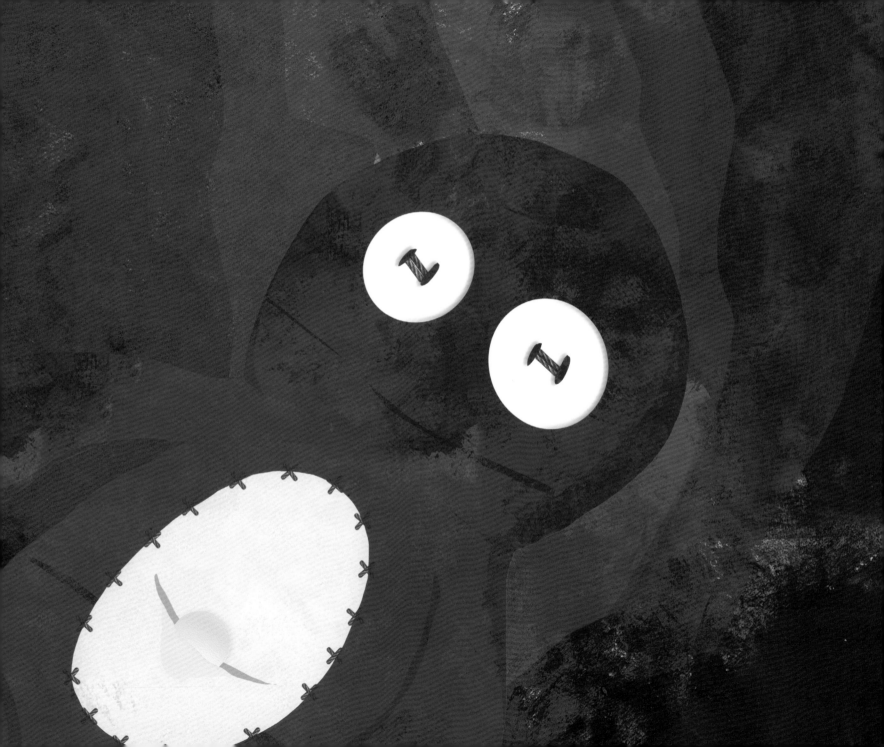

That day, the Stark found his joy.

*"Now, the Stark and Baby hunt for treasure together.*
*Baby rides in his daddy's pouch where it's warm and safe.*
*At night they watch the fire in the sunset."*

*"The Stark shoo shoos his little one to sleep."*

*"I'd like to see that cave sometime,"*
the little boy murmured.

He snuggled deeper into the folds of
his bed and closed his eyes.

*"Baby is the best treasure of all."*

# Cave Facts

### Cave

A *cave* is a hollow place in the ground, specifically a natural underground space large enough for a human to fit. The cave in the story is a karst cave.

### Crayfish

Michal Maňas [CC BY 2.5 (https://creativecommons.org/licenses/by/2.5)]

Cave insects and crustaceans who never venture outside usually have little pigmentation (white, pink or translucent) and are blind.

# Karst

*Karst* is a surface landscape composed of carbonate rocks such as limestone or gypsum. These are soluble rocks.

Rainwater or groundwater combines with carbon dioxide to form a weak acid. This acid slowly dissolves small amounts of calcium in the limestone. Water seeping into below-ground spaces loses the dissolved carbon dioxide to the air of the cave. Then the water can no longer hold as much calcium, and the extra is deposited on the ceiling, floor and walls of caves in the form of speleothems.

Karst exists all over the world. In the U.S., only Delaware and Rhode Island have no karst. Tennessee is rich in karst. Many soluble cave systems have been explored, or are still to be explored, there.

# Plinks and Plunks

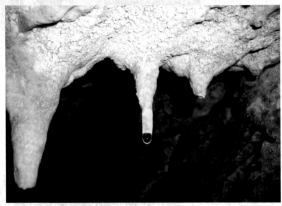

Sound bounces off the walls of a cave and produces an echo. The sounds of dripping water in a cave appear amplified in the stillness.

At times, a drop falling into the hollow tube compresses the air and produces a whistle.

# Speleothems

*Speleothems* are mineral deposits formed over vast periods of time from groundwater entering underground caverns. Speleothems made of pure *calcium carbonate* are a translucent white color. Natural chemicals or impurities add earthy tones. Speleothems can also be formed from salt, sulfur and other minerals.

Most of the observed cave features noted by the boy and the Stark are speleothems. The stone draperies, sea creatures, roses, the cave pearl and even the soda straws of the Stark's nest are formed from mineral deposits. Below is a description of those mentioned specifically in the story, although there are many more.

• Cave Pearls

A *cave pearl* is a round shape, similar to the pearl found in an oyster. A speck of sand rolls in moving water and picks up concentric layers of calcite over time. Some develop a polish. The cave pearl or oolite is a gift to the boy. Quite properly, the boy leaves it behind with the baby Stark.

• Columns

*Columns* form when a stalactite and a stalagmite grow into each other. Over time they can become very substantial. They are found in the palace.

- Drapery Formations (Curtains)

*Draperies* form as water slips between narrow cracks in the ceiling and evaporates before it falls, leaving mineral residue behind. The boy dips under these before entering the treasure palace.

- Flowstone

*Flowstone* is formed from water that does just that – flows. The calcite is deposited in thin layers which become smoother and rounder as they accumulate; hence, the reference to the whale's back.

- Gypsum Flowers

*Gypsum* is a fibrous mineral resulting when a calcium-sulphite solution feeds out through pores in the rock, sometimes pushing bits of the wall with it.Some gypsum can be flexible. In the story, the rose garden is a reference to gypsum formations that resemble flowers with curving petals.

- Helictites

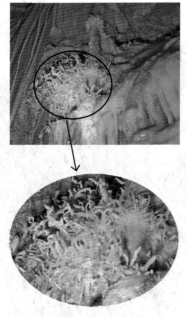

*Helictites* are stalactites that ignore gravity. They most often begin as soda straws that spiral and branch in all directions. Some resemble butterfly wings, stag antlers or even spider webs. They are the walrus whiskers in the story.

- Soda Straws

A *soda straw* is a very narrow stalactite. Soda straws are hollow and fragile. If the opening at the end of the tube becomes blocked, the soda straw will gradually widen and become a stalactite. In the story, soda straws provide the material of the Stark's nest.

- Stalactites

*Stalactites* are dripstones. They form slowly as water drips from the ceiling of the cave, leaving minerals behind. All stalactites start out as hollow tubes. In the story, they are the dragon teeth.

- Stalagmites

*Stalagmites* are formed when dripping water deposits minerals on the cave floor. Stalagmites are most often positioned directly underneath stalactites. They are also the dragon teeth of the story.

### The Author

**Ingrid Lee** is a writer of fiction and nonfiction for young people, whose books have been translated into multiple languages. When she is not writing or exploring, she teaches art and English.

### The Illustrator

**Johnny Hollick** is a mixed media artist and performer from Toronto. A graduate of the University of Toronto Fine Arts program, his projects have been featured in galleries and venues in a variety of forms, from traditional painting to multimedia performance. Presently his work is largely collage-based, generated digitally from textures, then reworked physically with scissors and wit.